PIG the TOURIST

Aaron Blabey

Scholastic Canada Ltd.
Toronto New York London Auckland Sydney
Mexico City New Delhi Hong Kong Buenos Aires

Pig was a Pug
and I'm sorry to say,
when he went on vacation
he'd cause great dismay.

AIRPORT EX
BAGGAGE CL

You could make careful plans
to ensure happy travel.
But Pig would destroy them.
He'd make them . . .

. . . unravel.

With behaviour so bad
it is hard to describe . . .

He would dampen
your trip . . .

and he'd ruin the vibe.

He'd break all the rules
and he'd flout all tradition.
Causing disaster
was Pig's big ambition.

Even in places
of wild celebration,
he'd somehow create
absolute devastation.

And if he could shatter
some ancient taboo —
he wouldn't think twice,
that appalling yahoo.

Parties, parades
and processions got wrecked
in a blizzard of chaos
and foul disrespect.

His insensitive antics
would ruin your stay,
till the locals would gather
and shout . . .

But that wouldn't stop him . . .

He'd rock . . .

MONA LISA ATTACKED!

The Louvre—Paris

Leonardo da Vinci's masterpiece was vandalized this morning in a brazen attack by an overweight dog with a tremendous sense of entitlement. Authorities believe he was working alone, but have detained a small dachshund for questioning. Monsieur Baguette of the Louvre security force made the following statement— "I do not like this dog."

NO NADAR!
NO SWIMMING!
PIRANHA!

Yes, if you treat locals
with little regard,
they'll come back to bite you . . .

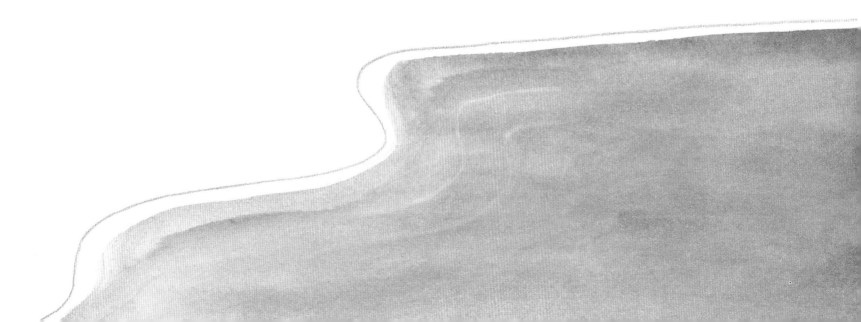

and boy, they bite hard.

These days it's different,
I'm happy to say.
He's learned not to ruin
a *whole* holiday.

But let us be honest.
The truth I must tell.
Although he might *try* . . .

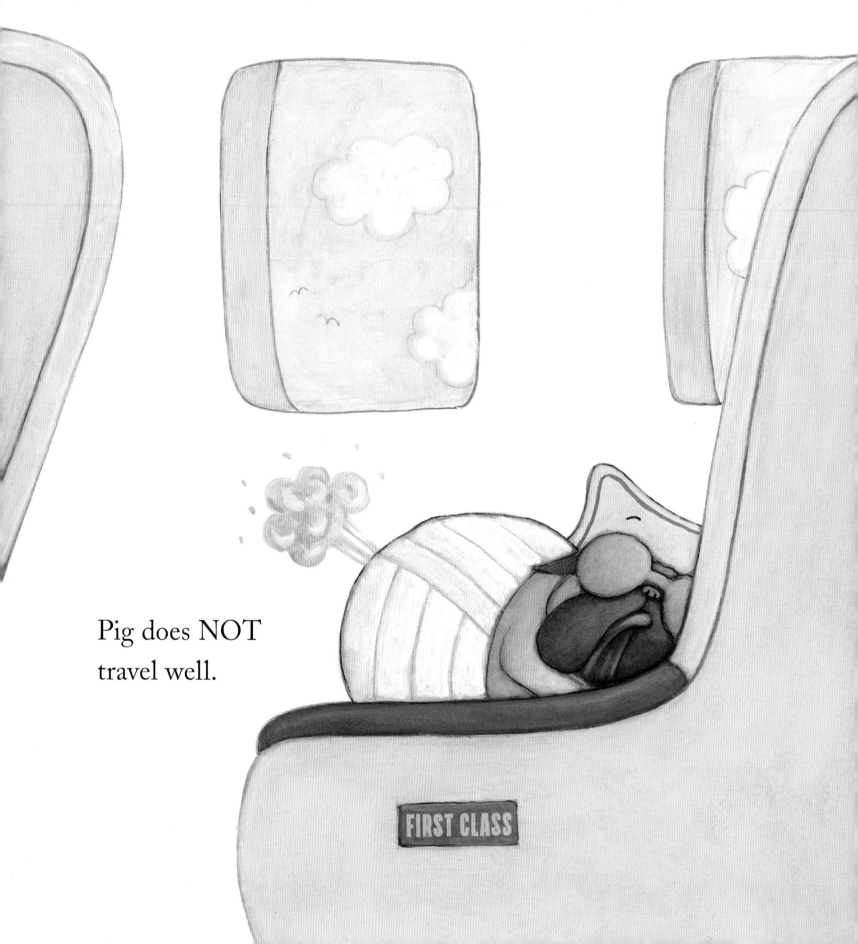

Pig does NOT travel well.

FIRST CLASS